Hoppy Birthday, Jo-Jo!

Pippa Goodhart

BoRE

D0293639

C0000 002 178 839

First published in Great Britain 2004
by Egmont Books Ltd
239 Kensington High Street, London W8 6SA
Text copyright © Pippa Goodhart 2004
Illustrations copyright © Georgie Birkett 2004
The author and illustrator have asserted their moral rights.
Paperback ISBN 1 4052 0874 0
10 9 8 7 6 5 4 3 2 1
A CIP catalogue record for this title is available from the British Library.
Printed in U.A.E.

This book is sold subject to the condition that it shall not, by way of trade or otherwise
be lent, resold, hired out, or otherwise circulated without the publisher's prior consent
in any form of binding or cover other than that in which it is published and without a
similar condition including this condition being imposed on the subsequent purchaser.

Pick a
Pocket

Hide-and-Seek
Cake

Hoppy
Birthday
Party

CZ178839 01/05

BRENTFORD LIBRARY

For the Australian Jo I know and love,
Josephine Clarke
P.G.

To Hannah and Kevan's new baby
(The Little Moose)
G.B.

Pick a Pocket

6

A new baby came to Jo-Jo's house.

'Jo-Jo, meet Baby Roo,' said Mum.

'That's MY pocket!' said Jo-Jo.

'You're too big for a pocket now,'

said Mum.

7

Baby Roo went in Jo-Jo's old cot.

'That's MY cot!' said Jo-Jo.

'You're too big for a cot,' said Dad.

'I'm not!' said Jo-Jo.

'Come and have a big-girl hug,'

said Mum.

'No hug!' said Jo-Jo.

'Do you want to help me plan your birthday party, Jo-Jo?' said Mum.

'No, no, no!' said Jo-Jo.

Mum and Dad went looking

for Jo-Jo.

She wasn't in the kitchen.

She wasn't in the garden.

She wasn't in her bedroom.

'Where are you, Jo-Jo?' they called.

14

At teatime Jo-Jo asked, 'Where is
Baby Roo?'

'Asleep. She is too little for buns.'

'Oh,' said Jo-Jo.

'Baby Roo is too little for lots of things,' said Mum. 'But you are big enough to have friends for a party.'

'Can it be a hide-and-seek party?'

said Jo-Jo.

Hooray!

'It can,' said Mum.

'Baby Roo can come to it too,'
said Jo-Jo.

Hide-and-Seek Cake

20

'It's my party today!' said Jo-Jo.

'Goo goo,' said Baby Roo.

'Let's make a cake,' said Mum.

They went to the shop. They got eggs and flour and sugar.

They got a big bag of sweets.

'Are they for my cake?' asked Jo-Jo.

'Yes,' said Mum.

Yummy!

Mum didn't cook the cake in a cake tin. She cooked it in a bowl.

Mum dug a hole in the cake.

Jo-Jo put icing and candles on the cake.

'No sweets on top,' said Mum.

Jo-Jo's party was in the garden.

'Where is everybody?' said Jo-Jo.

'Hiding,' said Mum. 'You must find them.'

Jo-Jo found Ted.

She found Ziggy.

She found Poppy.

They all found Wantab.

'Time for cake,' said Mum. 'Cut the hide-and-seek cake, Jo-Jo.'

31

Jo-Jo cut the cake. Lots of sweets

were hiding inside!

'Hoppy birthday to you, Jo-Jo!'

Hoppy
Birthday
Party

Jo-Jo and Poppy and Ted and Ziggy and Wantab played party games.

Hopscotch. Jumping in sacks.

And jumping for apples.

They played pick a pocket.

37

'Time for presents,' said Dad.

'I can't see any presents,' said Jo-Jo.

'You have to find them!' said Dad.

Jo-Jo looked to the left.

She looked to the right.

'Look up,' said Mum.

Jo-Jo picked a banana, and

opened it.

Ooooh!

'Look down,' said Dad.

'The red flower!' said Jo-Jo.

It's a teddy!

'Our present is too big to be wrapped,' said Dad. 'So I will wrap you up instead, Jo-Jo!'

Dad led Jo-Jo into the house.

'Now look!' said Dad.

'A new room! All for me! And with a bunk bed!' said Jo-Jo. 'Oh, thank you!'

They all played jumping to catch the stars until it was time to go home.

'I like being a big girl,' said Jo-Jo.

'And I do like Baby Roo.'

'Good,' said Mum.

'Goo,' said Baby Roo.